Striped Shirts
and
Flowered Pants

To Diane Louise Smithwick Schnurbush,
loving daughter, sister, wife, mother, and nana–BS

To the families and their loved ones
with Alzheimer's disease–CP

Published by
MAGINATION PRESS
An Educational Publishing Foundation Book
American Psychological Association
750 First Street, NE
Washington, DC 20002

For more information about our books, including a complete catalog, please write to us, call 1-800-374-2721, or visit our website at www.maginationpress.com.

Managing Editor: Darcie Johnston
Project Editor: Kristine Enderle
Art Director: Susan K. White
Printed by Worzalla, Stevens Point, Wisconsin

Library of Congress Cataloging-in-Publication Data

Schnurbush, Barbara.
Striped shirts and flowered pants : a story about Alzheimer's disease
for young children / by Barbara Schnurbush ; illustrated by Cary Pillo.
p. cm.
ISBN-13: 978-1-59147-475-3 (hardccover : alk. paper)
ISBN-10: 1-59147-475-2 (hardccover : alk. paper)
ISBN-13: 978-1-59147-476-0 (pbk. : alk. paper)
ISBN-10: 1-59147-476-0 (pbk. : alk. paper)
1. Alzheimer's disease--Juvenile literature. I. Pillo, Cary. II. Title.
C523.3.S36 2007
618.92'831—dc22   2006009605

10 9 8 7 6 5 4 3 2 1

Striped Shirts and Flowered Pants

A STORY ABOUT ALZHEIMER'S DISEASE FOR YOUNG CHILDREN

by Barbara Schnurbush

illustrated by Cary Pillo

MAGINATION PRESS • WASHINGTON, D.C.

Nana is lots of fun.
Sometimes we read
stories together.

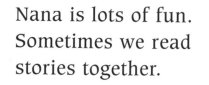

We make pictures
of flowers and
happy faces.
Nana likes to
color too.

Sometimes we
watch TV together.
Nana laughs almost
as much as I do.

In the spring, we plant flowers
in the garden.
Nana loves sunflowers the best.

When it's sunny, we go outside
and listen to birds.
Nana knows about birds and
tells me all the different kinds.

One day, Mom noticed that
Nana's clothes didn't match.
It didn't bother me. My favorite
outfit is my blue striped shirt
with my orange flowered pants.
Grown-ups always think *it*
doesn't match either.

Another day, Nana had trouble saying
some words in the book she was reading
to me. So we looked at the pictures and
talked about the story instead.

And one day, Nana couldn't remember
the name of her favorite bird.
I reminded her that it was called a chickadee.
I guess she got a little mixed up.

After that, I heard everyone talking about Nana.
Daddy said she was forgetting lots of things.
Mommy talked about Nana's clothes not matching.

Grampa was worried about Nana too.
He said that Nana left the stove on
after she cooked macaroni and cheese.

I asked Mommy and Daddy
if there was something wrong with Nana.
I didn't want Nana to burn her house down.

I wondered if she was sick. I was afraid she might die.

Daddy said that Nana would live a long time, but her brain wasn't working right. Her brain wasn't telling her how to do things.

Mommy said that doctors can fix a sore tummy or a broken arm, but they can't fix Nana's brain or help her remember things.

They said someday she might need to come live with us or have someone like a nurse help take care of her.

I wondered if Nana knew
that sometimes she forgot
the words in my books.

Did she know that
sometimes her clothes
didn't match?

Did she know
about the macaroni?

I got scared.
Sometimes my clothes
don't match.
I wondered if
there was something wrong
with my brain too.

People with Alzheimer's disease can get really confused too.
Nana might take a walk and then forget where she is.
Mommy said that she will need to keep an eye on her
so she won't get lost.

Some people with Alzheimer's disease might be happy, then all of a sudden get mad.

Daddy said if that happens he'll talk quietly to Nana until she calms down.

Now I know that Nana doesn't always
remember how to do things or how to act
because she has Alzheimer's disease.
But there are lots of ways I can help Nana too.

When Nana looks sad, I give her a hug.

Or sometimes we go into the garden and
fill up the bird feeders with sunflower seeds.
Birds fly in from everywhere!
That makes her smile.

If Nana acts mad at me, even though I didn't do anything wrong, I find Grampa. He can make her calm. Sometimes she just needs to take some quiet time.

In the spring, I went to Nana's house to help her plant flowers.
We planted red and blue ones, purple ones, and orange ones,
just like the ones we grew last year.

We also planted lots of sunflowers.

Nana asked me to remember
to water the flowers so they
would grow big and healthy.

We sat at the picnic table and watched birds
flying around the bird feeders.
Nana looked at me and then gave me a big hug.

She whispered in my ear, "Libby, please don't
ever forget how much I love you."

"I won't," I whispered back.
"I love you forever too, Nana."

I can help Nana
and show her
all the things I've
learned from her
and even help her
read my books.

I can talk to Mommy and Daddy when I'm feeling sad
or worried about Nana. We have lots of love in our family,
and that helps us all work together.

And Nana and I can both wear
striped shirts and flowered pants,
and it will be okay.

Note to Parents

When a grandparent (or other family member) has Alzheimer's disease, children in the family usually need help understanding what's happening and coping with their feelings. They may feel confused, sad, worried, embarrassed, and angry in the face of their grandparent's odd behavior, especially if the grandparent and the child have enjoyed a close relationship.

Understanding the psychological issues that confront a young child and finding ways to talk about feelings and problems can help parents significantly reduce their child's distress. Children do best when they are encouraged to talk about what's on their minds. Your child may be wondering:

Why is Grandpa acting this way?

Why is he so angry?

Why does Grandma ask the same question over and over?

Why does she act like a kid?

Why can't Grandpa take care of himself?

Will you get Alzheimer's disease too, like Grandma?

Using language that is age-appropriate, provide the information that your children need. It may be helpful to do some research or seek additional information from your family physician to clarify your understanding of the disease and how it affects families. Be ready to respond to questions and feelings that emerge, while at the same time being careful not to overwhelm your children with more information than necessary. Simple explanations are best.

EXPLAIN THE DISEASE

Alzheimer's disease is a progressive brain disorder that affects a person's memory, reasoning, and ability to communicate, and often personality and behavior as well. Again, a simple, age-appropriate explanation is best. You might begin by saying, "Grandma has an illness called Alzheimer's disease. It's a disease in the brain, but it's not the kind of disease that we can catch from each other, like the flu. It happens sometimes when people get very old. It affects the way people think and feel. That's why Grandma forgets things and acts differently sometimes." Reading this story will also help explain what your children might expect as the disease progresses.

Personality and behavior changes are the most troubling for a child (and adults) to witness, especially if the grandparent's behavior is aggressive or delusional. As much as possible, protect children when a grandparent is behaving aggressively or experiencing a delusion. Remove them from the situation in a matter-of-fact way and help them emotionally navigate what they just saw, using a simple statement such as, "Grandma's brain isn't working correctly right now. That's why she's yelling at the TV. Why don't you go play in your room for a few minutes while I help Grandma calm down?"

DESCRIBE YOUR ROLE AS CAREGIVER

A person with Alzheimer's disease will usually live many years after symptoms become noticeable. Often much of that time is spent under the care of a spouse, relatives, or friends. To prepare your child for your new role as caregiver, explain that the grandparent can't take care of himself the way he used to and needs your help. You may need to assist with bathing, dressing, and cooking. You will likely go on doctor's appointments with the grandparent. Later on, you may make frequent visits to residential and assisted living centers.

Your children may feel displaced or ignored, or resent sharing you with someone who places such demands on you. Allow them to express these negative feelings to you. It is also important that you regularly set aside time to spend with them, so that they know they are safe and loved–an important part of the family. At the same time, it's best to maintain the same rules, rituals, and schedules that you had before, so that their world stays as predictable and stable as possible.

HELP CHILDREN IDENTIFY THEIR FEELINGS

Parents can do a lot to help their children cope with feelings of sadness, anger, resentment, frustration, confusion, guilt, and fear. Talking about the feelings allows a child to identify them and to begin to work through them, especially when they are feeling several conflicting emotions at the same time. Reassure your child that all of these feelings are normal.

For example, you might say, "It's okay to feel mad at Grandpa sometimes. It doesn't mean you don't love him. Most kids would feel that way if their grandparent acted the way Grandpa just did." Or "It's completely understandable that you're unhappy about the amount of time I need to spend with Grandma. It doesn't mean you don't love her or don't want me to spend time with her. But it does mean I don't get to spend as much time with you, and this is a big change for all of us that we weren't expecting. I know we will all adjust fine, but promise me you'll let me know when something is really on your mind or you need to spend some time with me."

It is natural for children to feel angry when things get rough. They may get frustrated with the grandparent if they have to repeat activities or answer the same questions again and again. Empathize with their frustration, and commend them when they demonstrate patience with the grandparent or practice good listening skills. You may say, "I know it can get frustrating when Grandma can't find the right word to say or repeats the same question over and over. The way you took the time to listen is very helpful and supportive. I appreciate that, and so does she."

If possible, grandparents can also offer reassurance that they are still the same person, and that they still care for and love the child, despite their sometimes confusing or upsetting behavior.

PLAN SIMPLE AND FUN ACTIVITIES

Basic chores and routine tasks like folding clothes or putting away groceries might help children interact with their grandparent in a comfortable and positive way. Other activities could include listening to music, reading together, or looking at photographs. While a grandparent is able, encourage your child to connect this way. It could be a rewarding experience for both the child and grandparent.

If your child resists or avoids spending time with the grandparent, you might say, "I know it's hard to see Grandpa acting differently or being so forgetful. Let's think of ways we can make it easier for you to be together. Do you have any ideas?" Build on your child's ideas, or offer some of your own, such as making visits shorter, inviting Grandpa to the child's soccer game, or watching TV or a movie so that the two of them can be together without having to talk so much.

TAKE TIME FOR COMFORT AND SUPPORT

Children need extra comfort and support when a grandparent's behavior gets upsetting or incomprehensible. A child may not be able to adjust smoothly to each change that Alzheimer's disease brings. It may help to say that Grandpa is behaving unusually because of the disease and not because he doesn't care for or love the child. Be careful, though, not to imply that the child's feelings are invalid.

Also, most children are afraid of illness in parents and grandparents. They may wonder if you will get Alzheimer's or when you might die. If this is troubling your child, you might say, "I am wondering if you're worried that your dad or I will get Alzheimer's disease or die. Usually people don't get Alzheimer's or die until they are very, very old and sick. We are young and healthy, and we plan to stay that way for a long, long time. We work hard to take care of ourselves, so you don't need to worry about us."

SEEK RELIEF AND RESPITE CARE

Parents may find themselves sandwiched between care-giving responsibilities for their children and their own parents. With such added responsibility, it is important that you find time for rest and relaxation for yourself, and perhaps seek respite care, as needed. This is not only good for you but good for your entire family. Respite care allows you to take a break while the person with Alzheimer's receives care from friends, other family members, volunteers, or a professional caregiver. You could use respite care services when you need to spend some time with your child, run errands, or have some time to yourself.

Find organized support and resources. The Alzheimer's Association (800-272-3900; www.alz.org) has a national network of local chapters. These chapters provide information and support to families in a variety of ways. Chapters often have a telephone helpline, support groups, lending libraries, and other education services for families and people with Alzheimer's. Chapters also are a good source for community services such as home care, respite services, adult day care, assisted living or skilled nursing facilities, eldercare lawyers, financial planners, and transportation.

Linda Scacco, Ph.D., is a clinical psychologist, an adjunct professor at the University of Hartford, and the author of Always My Grandpa, *a children's story about Alzheimer's disease. She lives in Connecticut with her family.*

About the Author

BARBARA SCHNURBUSH lives in New Hampshire with her husband and three children. Her own experiences with both a grandparent and a parent prompted her to write this book to help families coping with Alzheimer's disease.

About the Illustrator

CARY PILLO grew up on a farm near the Cascade Mountains in Washington State, and now lives in Seattle with her husband and son and their dog Atlas. She has illustrated many children's books, including *A Terrible Thing Happened*, *Gentle Willow*, and *Tibby Tried It*.